Sir Walter Scott's
IVANHOE

ADAPTED BY MARIANNA MAYER

PAINTINGS BY JOHN RUSH

chronicle books · san francisco

Book design by John Rush and April Ward.
Typeset in Adobe Jensen.
The illustrations in this book were rendered in oil on canvas.
Leather cover artwork created by Scott K. Kellar Bookbinding & Conservation.
Manufactured in China.

ISBN 1-58717-248-8 (hardcover)
ISBN 1-58717-249-6 (library edition)

Library of Congress Cataloging-in-Publication Data available.

Distributed in Canada by Raincoast Books
9050 Shaughnessy Street, Vancouver, British Columbia V6P 6E5

10 9 8 7 6 5 4 3 2 1

Chronicle Books LLC
85 Second Street, San Francisco, California 94105

www.chroniclekids.com

For Bill Le Moine and his beloved daughter Chelsea
—M. M.

To the spirit of chivalry
—J. R.

scotland

ireland

england

wales

york
sheffield

london

normandy

N

ANNO · DOMINI · 1192

NEARLY ONE HUNDRED YEARS *had passed since the Duke of Normandy conquered Anglo-Saxon England at the Battle of Hastings in 1066. But in all that time, the hatred between the victorious Normans and the defeated Saxons had only deepened.*

When King Richard the Lion-Hearted took the throne in 1160, though he himself was a Norman, he tried to unite the two rival clans so that Saxons and Normans alike might live in peace as Englishmen. But Richard left his kingdom to join the Crusades, and in his absence much turmoil followed. His brother, Prince John, seized the throne and declared himself acting regent. Hoping never to surrender the crown to his brother, John curried favor with the Normans by abusing the rights of the Saxons. For if King Richard was for England, John was for John.

CAST OF CHARACTERS

NORMANS

Prior Aymer

Sir Brian de Bois-Guilbert

Prince John

King Richard the Lion-Hearted

Sir Front-de-Boeuf

Sir De Bracy

Sir Philip de Malvoisin

Sir de Grantmesnil

The Grand Master of the Templars

The Abbot of Templestowe

SAXONS

Cedric the Saxon

Princess Rowena, Cedric's ward

Wilfred of Ivanhoe
(Sir Desdichado)

Prince Athelstane

Wamba, the jester

Ulrica

OTHERS

Isaac of York

Rebecca of York

Locksley of Sherwood Forest
(Robin Hood)

Friar Tuck

IX

O N THE NIGHT BEFORE a royal tournament, a party of Normans rode through the dark forest en route to the festive event. But a sudden rainstorm sent them hurrying instead to Cedric the Saxon's nearby estate, Rotherwood, in search of shelter.

Among them, a portly and all-too-worldly abbot named Prior Aymer observed, "This Cedric is an arrogant Saxon. He stubbornly clings to his clan's ancient customs and their old line of kings. But we shall feast well tonight, for he is also known for his splendid table and good ale."

"And his ward, Princess Rowena, is beautiful, I am told," added Sir Brian de Bois-Guilbert, a handsome, determined man in his prime. Hailed as the finest champion of the Knights of Templar, he had only recently returned from the Crusades.

"Beware, Guilbert," cautioned the abbot. "Cedric will not take kindly to your interest in that princess. He banished his own son and heir, Wilfred of Ivanhoe, for the crime of loving her. Rowena is promised to Athelstane, the last prince in the line of Saxon kings."

"Ivanhoe," said Guilbert darkly. A deep scar on his brow gave a sinister cast to one eye. "He fought beside me in the Crusades. He is dead, and just as well."

A few moments later, they reached the crossroads, and Guilbert called out, "Are we to go left or right?"

As the abbot hesitated, he spied a shadowy figure standing near a tree. "You, there!" he called out. "Which way to Cedric the Saxon's castle?"

Dressed in the dark cape and hat of a simple pilgrim, the stranger stepped forward. "It is to the right. I know the path well."

"Good, then you will guide us," said the abbot.

SHORT WHILE LATER, they entered Rotherwood, Cedric's noble castle. Though forced to be hospitable, Cedric was none too pleased to have Normans at his table.

"What say you of the Crusades, Guilbert?" asked Cedric when his guests were seated.

"The Holy Order of the Templar Knights continues to further our cause in Palestine," Guilbert answered. But his glances were for Rowena, for though as a Templar he had taken solemn vows never to wed, he was not above a flirtation with a pretty maiden.

"Are there no Saxons worthy of mention, sir?" asked Rowena, hoping for news of Ivanhoe, whom she deeply loved, even if she was promised to another.

"The Saxons were second only to the Templars, lady," answered Guilbert.

Sitting quietly by the fire with his back to the others was the pilgrim. At Guilbert's words he turned and said, "The Saxons were second to none. I myself am recently returned from Palestine, and while there I saw one Saxon knight meet you stroke for stroke on the battlefield."

Cedric looked sharply at the Templar. "Has this Saxon a name?"

XIII

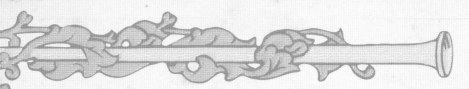

"It was Ivanhoe," replied Guilbert with a sneer. "And were he alive today, I would challenge him to see who is the better knight."

"Ivanhoe, dead! I will not believe it. If I were a man, I would accept your challenge in his name," cried Rowena, half rising from her seat before Cedric stopped her.

"If Ivanhoe is dead, sir, it is only your word that says it is so," noted the pilgrim.

Ignoring him, Guilbert bowed his head with a charming smile to Rowena, saying, "I for one am glad you are not a man, lady."

At that moment, a servant announced a new guest. "Isaac of York, the merchant Jew, seeks shelter from the storm, master."

"Have him enter and take warmth from our fire," said Cedric.

"Would you welcome an unbeliever into our midst?" asked the indignant abbot.

"You above all should know that tonight my castle is open to those in need," Cedric answered pointedly. After acknowledging his host's hospitality, the merchant gratefully took the place offered him at the hearth beside the pilgrim, keeping well away from the others.

WHEN THE DINNER was over and the guests began to leave the hall, only the pilgrim hung back. Quickly, he stepped into the shadows and waited for Princess Rowena to pass. As she did, he grasped her hand and pulled her into the darkness.

Removing the hat that concealed his face, he asked, "Have I changed so much, my lady?"

"Ivanhoe!" Rowena gasped. "I knew you could not be dead! Let us not waste a moment. If we flee at once it will be hours before they discover I've gone."

"No," said Ivanhoe, kissing her hands. "I will not have us steal away like criminals, only to be hunted down later. When I've proven myself, then will I face my father and plead our cause. I will beg if I have to, but I will make him see that we must be together."

Reluctantly Rowena nodded, knowing in her heart that Ivanhoe spoke wisely.

As HE PARTED from Rowena, Ivanhoe assumed his disguise once more, and then slipped away down the corridor. On the way to find his sleeping quarters, he overheard whispering. It was

Guilbert's men, plotting to kill Isaac the merchant and steal his money.

Quietly, Ivahoe went to the barn where Isaac slept and woke him. "You are in grave danger, merchant," he whispered. "Come, I will help you escape!"

But as the two made ready, they were attacked. In the dark, one villain threw Isaac to the ground as another tried to strangle him. Without benefit of a sword, Ivanhoe seized upon a pole and swiftly dispatched both assassins.

Once Isaac and Ivanhoe were safely away from the castle, the older man said, "It's clear that you are no pilgrim, but a knight in sorry need of a fine warhorse and armor. Please allow me to repay

you for saving my life. I will gladly lend you both once we reach my home. Then you could compete at the grand tournament tomorrow. Am I wrong in guessing that this is your wish?"

"You seem able to read my mind, Isaac," admitted Ivanhoe. "A chance at the tournament tomorrow would allow me to settle a score with a certain Templar knight."

 HEN THE DAY of the tournament arrived, among the many Saxon and Norman spectators were Cedric and Rowena, and with them was her betrothed prince, Athelstane. Isaac of York was also there, with his beautiful daughter, Rebecca, known to be a gifted healer.

Prince John hosted the popular event, and gave the signal for the tournament to begin. Five Norman knights, led by Sir Brian de Bois-Guilbert, rode forward, and five Saxon knights took up the challenge. Trumpets sounded, and at full gallop the knights and their mounts rode out against each other. Lances and shields clashed, and the Templar and his fellow knights took the victory. A second group of Saxon knights rode onto the field, and they, too, were quickly vanquished by the Normans. And following this twice more the Saxons were sorely beaten.

Too old to fight, Cedric struck his fist in frustration, saying to his ward, "Is there no one to uphold the Saxon honor this day?"

Just then a solitary trumpet sounded, heralding a new champion to the field. All eyes turned to see a knight in brilliant armor inlaid

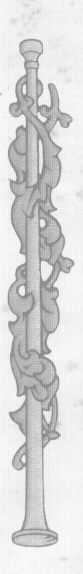

with gold. His shield was emblazoned with the mysterious sign of a young oak tree pulled up by its roots, inscribed only with the Spanish word *Desdichado*, the Disinherited.

"Sir Knight," instructed Prince John, "choose your adversary by the stroke of your lance upon his shield."

On a gallant black horse, the knight rode by and struck Guilbert's shield so hard with his lance that it shattered.

"A challenge for combat to the death," observed Isaac in surprise.

Then, with the sharp point of his lance, the knight lightly tapped the shields of the other four Norman knights, challenging them to joust with him.

"He defies all five!" exclaimed Rebecca.

The crowd went wild at such daring, and Guilbert set out first to face the new opponent alone. Through clenched teeth, Guilbert said, "Pray you are ready to meet your Maker, sir."

"I am more ready than you, Templar, for my conscience is clear," replied the stranger.

The trumpet sounded once more, and the two rode at each other. Like a thunderbolt they met head-on, splitting their lances. Turning back only to receive fresh weapons, they again charged. This time Guilbert was hurled from his horse. Enraged, he sprang to his feet and drew his sword. Just as the two rushed at each other, an attendant rode onto the field, declaring Sir Desdichado the victor for that round.

"We shall meet again," said Guilbert.

XIX

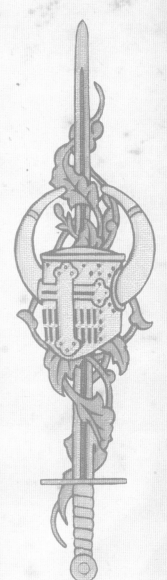

Now the remaining four Norman knights rode out one by one to answer the newcomer. Sir Front-de-Boeuf, Sir De Bracy, Sir Philip de Malvoisin, and Sir de Grantmesnil followed one another in quick succession, as Sir Desdichado astonishingly bested them all.

Prince John, who clearly favored the Normans, reluctantly proclaimed the victor amidst the cheering crowd. "You, Sir Desdichado, have won the right to choose the Queen of Love and Beauty. Which of our lovely ladies will you honor?"

The champion received the crown and rode to where Rowena was seated. "Hail, the Saxon princess, Rowena, as the Queen of Love and Beauty," shouted the Saxon spectators with pride.

Furious, Prince John announced the rules for the second round. "Two equal groups are to meet in general combat. At the close of the events, the Queen of Love and Beauty will crown the knight deemed victor." Under his breath he said to his advisor, "Now, may this Sir Desdichado and his Saxon friends get what they deserve."

Two bands rode out onto the field, one group led by Desdichado, the other by Guilbert. Almost at once, what was to be good sport turned brutal. Those Saxons who fell were savagely attacked with swords as well as daggers.

"Daggers!" said Isaac to his daughter, Rebecca. "This is not right. John must call a halt."

Soon the field was littered with the dead and wounded. Appalled, Prince John's advisor whispered, "Stop the fight, sire. This is not a tournament, but a massacre."

But John only gave him an evil smile.

Desdichado and Guilbert were bitterly pitted against each other, and appeared an even match. But then three Norman knights came to fight beside Guilbert. Suddenly, out of nowhere, a lone Black Knight rode to Desdichado's side to even the odds. The others were no match for him and Desdichado. Together they dropped one Norman knight after another, giving each a mighty blow, and then Desdichado turned back to continue his fight with Guilbert. Only then did Prince John rise to end the combat. At that same moment, the Black Knight took this as his cue to leave the field and quickly disappeared.

XXI

Prince John had no choice but to name the disinherited knight victor. But as Rowena started to place the laurel wreath upon the champion's head, the prince insisted, "The knight's helmet must be removed to receive the honor."

The helmet was lifted off, revealing the face of Ivanhoe. But then Ivanhoe collapsed at Rowena's feet, senseless.

Rowena implored Cedric to help, but, turning away, Cedric replied, "I have no son."

Across the field, Rebecca gasped. "Quickly!" she cried to those beside her, "I am a physician. Carry him to my wagon."

Heeding her plea, a group of woodsmen rushed onto the field and lifted the wounded man. As they placed the unconscious man in Rebecca's wagon, Isaac said, "I fear we are involving ourselves in a dangerous mission of mercy."

"After he saved your life! We cannot now leave him to die, Father," Rebecca insisted.

AT THE CLOSE of the tournament, Guilbert's wounded pride made him eager to seek revenge against Ivanhoe, as well as the other Saxons. He had a plan, but he could not execute it alone. First he took De Bracy aside and said, "I know well enough that you fancy the Princess Rowena."

"Is it so obvious?" De Bracy answered, his cheeks flushing with embarrassment. "But the Saxon princess and her guardian would never consider me a likely husband."

"Not unless you distinguished yourself," replied Guilbert.

XXIII

"How should I do that?" De Bracy inquired with a laugh.

Pausing only long enough to be assured that they would not be overheard, Guilbert proposed that they and the other knights whom Ivanhoe had defeated disguise themselves as outlaws. They would lay in wait in the forest and capture Rowena while she was journeying with Cedric to Rotherwood. Once the Normans were safely away with their prize, De Bracy could leave them. Then, assuming his true identity, he should dash back to rescue Rowena single-handedly, while her captors displayed mock resistance.

Fresh from their staggering defeat at the hands of Ivanhoe, the other knights readily agreed, hoping for some sport where they might easily triumph at the Saxons' expense. Yet De Bracy hesitated, agreeing only after the others promised that there would be no bloodshed.

At the same time Isaac, Rebecca, and her patient, Ivanhoe, began their journey home through the same forest. But on their way, the wheel of their wagon broke loose, leaving them stranded. Presently, along the road came Cedric and his ward, accompanied by their attendants as well as Wamba, the jester. "It seems you are in need of assistance, merchant," said Cedric as he directed his men to repair the wagon.

No sooner had they begun to help than, without warning, a band of masked outlaws burst out of the wood and attacked. In the midst of screams and shouts, de-Boeuf, who loved killing best of all, raised his sword to slay Cedric. Seeing this, De Bracy rushed to save

XXIV

Cedric, shouting, "No bloodshed!" and was promptly unmasked in the struggle.

"You fools," exclaimed Guilbert as he removed his own mask. "Now our plot is ruined."

"We have no choice but to hold them for ransom at my nearby fortress," reasoned de-Boeuf. "The Saxon clan will pay dearly for Cedric and his ward. And the merchant's own treasure will provide for his and his daughter's freedom. At least we shall get gold for our trouble!"

When the captives were secured, De Bracy gladly took charge of Princess Rowena. At the same time, Guilbert saw to it that he alone carried away the fair Rebecca, leaving the rest to be led by de-Boeuf and the others.

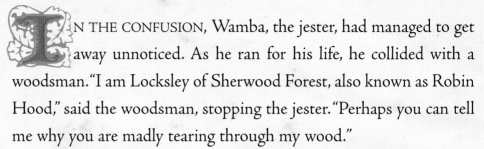

IN THE CONFUSION, Wamba, the jester, had managed to get away unnoticed. As he ran for his life, he collided with a woodsman. "I am Locksley of Sherwood Forest, also known as Robin Hood," said the woodsman, stopping the jester. "Perhaps you can tell me why you are madly tearing through my wood."

Struggling to catch his breath, Wamba at last told his tale and declared he was going to rescue the others.

"Without weapons or skill? Amazing!" said Robin with a laugh. "Then I suppose you have no need of help."

"Oh, yes, yes!" shouted Wamba. "I would be most grateful."

"Well, it is help you shall get from me and my band of outlaws," Robin declared. "I have no love for the Normans, for they tax the poor to get richer and wish to claim this forest for their own." Then he gave a sharp whistle, and all at once they were surrounded by many men dressed like their leader.

"Men, honest Saxons have been kidnapped in our forest," said Robin. "Go gather our companions, and I'll fetch Friar Tuck to join us. We shall bring all our forces down on the villains responsible."

Taking Wamba with him, Robin soon arrived at the friar's shelter. When Friar Tuck opened the door, behind him stood the towering figure of the Black Knight who had fought beside Ivanhoe at the tournament. When Robin explained what was afoot, the knight shook his head and said, "Is this what has become of England in my absence? Knights who should uphold honor now have turned into thieves and oppressors!"

"As they have always been," said the friar.

The Black Knight frowned. "There must be an end to such crimes," he said. "I will do whatever I can to help in the rescue."

At DE-BOEUF'S CASTLE, the prisoners were separated. Still unconscious, Ivanhoe was left unaided in a chamber, and Isaac was thrown into the dungeon. "You will tell me where you hide your gold, merchant," said de-Boeuf. "Or you'll suffer a long and painful death, roasting like a joint of beef on a spit over the fire."

"I will tell you nothing unless my daughter is released," said the old man.

"Are you mad?" asked de-Boeuf. "Do you think you have charms

against such torture? Get the fire ready!" de-Boeuf shouted to his men before storming out.

A T THE SAME TIME, De Bracy brought Rowena to a royal chamber. "Please be seated, my lady," he said with a courtly bow.

"Sir, after kidnapping me, do you dare to treat me as a suitor would?" asked Rowena.

"It is true, my lady," De Bracy confessed. "I hope to win your heart."

"Be advised, sir. You are off to a very bad start," replied Rowena.

If De Bracy hoped for a chance to change Rowena's mind, his friend Guilbert harbored his own romantic hopes regarding the beautiful Rebecca, for from the moment he saw her he felt compelled to win her. After taking Rebecca to a private chamber, Guilbert said, "Lady, you have nothing to fear from me."

Rebecca observed him carefully and saw the Templar cross sewn upon his tunic. "You are no outlaw," said she. "Do you not care that by your conduct today you have dishonored yourself and your holy order as a Templar knight?"

"That may be, Rebecca, but I will gladly dishonor such vows for the love of you," Guilbert replied, coming toward her.

"I would rather die!" cried Rebecca, flinging the shutters to the window open. In an instant she stood upon the parapet with nothing between her and the ground far below. "I will jump if you come one step closer."

XXIX

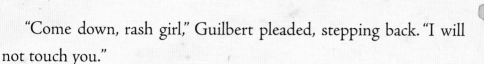

"Come down, rash girl," Guilbert pleaded, stepping back. "I will not touch you."

"I do not believe such a promise from you, sir," answered Rebecca.

"I will not break my word to you," Guilbert insisted.

Rebecca stepped down, but remained near the window. "Why should I believe you?"

"I will not force you to love me," he assured her. "Seeing your fierceness and courage only makes me wish for your love on your own terms or not at all."

Before she could reply, shouts were heard from below announcing a visitor. Guilbert left her to see who it might be. At the gate, he found de-Boeuf and De Bracy talking with the gatekeeper. "A letter has just arrived. Read it," said de-Boeuf, who could not read.

Guilbert quickly read the letter, "'You have seized our master and other persons. We demand that all of them be released or we will storm the castle. Signed, Wamba, the fool.'"

"What do we have to fear from a jester!" said de-Boeuf with a laugh.

"Nothing," answered Guilbert. "But there may be more to this than what appears. And, if so, we will need help. We shall send a reply stating that we will execute the prisoners one by one unless our ransom is paid. Meanwhile, this jester may send a priest to give the last rites. When the priest is finished with the prisoners, we shall send

XXXI

him away on our own errand. He shall be given a sealed message to be delivered to our friend, Philip de Malvoisin, asking for aid."

ARLY THE NEXT DAY, the Normans' ultimatum was answered by the appearance of a figure wearing priestly robes. "I have come to give the prisoners the last rites," said the priest.

After a guard took him to Cedric's cell and left them alone, the priest removed the hood of his robe. "Wamba!" exclaimed Cedric.

"Aye, master. It is your trusty fool," said Wamba. "Quickly, now, put on these robes and be off."

"I will not let a fool die in my place," declared Cedric.

"Master, believe me, I do not expect to die any time soon. And, to ensure that neither of us does, your skill is needed."

"Is there truly a chance for rescue then?" asked the old Saxon.

"Aye, master," answered Wamba. "Five hundred men now await you in the forest."

And so Cedric put on the priestly disguise and hurried to leave the castle. But he was stopped abruptly by an old woman. "You are no priest!" she cried out.

"And who are you?" asked Cedric.

"Ha! You do not recognize me. Yet you know me, Cedric. I am Ulrica, once the mistress of this castle. Do you not recall that as a girl you courted me? But that was long before the Normans seized

XXXII

this place. For so many years I've remained here as their slave that I'd almost forgotten the life I once had. Now, seeing you brings it all back and gives me the will to fight.

"Now, listen, for I have a plan," continued Ulrica. "Lead your forces to attack the north wall and the castle gates. When you see a red flag above the castle's turret, press your advantage, for by then there will be as much for the Normans to do within as without."

Thanking her, Cedric embraced the old woman and set out once more. But just as he was about to pass through the gates, he was stopped again. "Halt!" said a voice. "Go no further." It was Guilbert. "Carry this letter to the castle of Philip de Malvoisin, and be careful you are not stopped along the way."

"As you wish, my son," answered Cedric from behind the hood of his robe.

AS SOON AS the rescue party saw that Cedric was safely past the gates, they attacked. But the castle was well fortified. A high wall surrounded it, giving a first line of defense against intruders. Beyond this barrier and its gates was a moat, and unless the drawbridge could be lowered, there was no way to gain entry.

Soon the shouts of men and the hiss of arrows filled the air. The Black Knight led the attack on the barriers, while Cedric and Locksley brought a battering ram to break through the gates. As the gates gave way, de-Boeuf met the intruders on the other side with sword in hand. He and the Black Knight fought, and the Black

XXXIV

Knight fell, his sword broken. In an instant he was on his feet again, now wielding an ax. De-Boeuf took a mortal blow and went down.

At last, only the moat separated the rescuers from access to the castle.

MEANWHILE, Ulrica was setting fires inside the castle. When she reached Rebecca's room, she unlocked the door. "Your patient is much in need of you, lady," she said.

"Where is he?" cried Rebecca. "Please let me see him."

The old woman took her to Ivanhoe's cell and left her. Terribly weak from loss of blood, Ivanhoe could barely lift his head to speak. "For pity's sake, Rebecca, save yourself. There is no hope for me."

"I will not leave you," she vowed. "We will be saved or we will perish together."

"You are as brave as any knight I have ever met, and more beautiful than . . .," Ivanhoe began.

But Rebecca put a slender finger to his lips to silence him, and said, "Hush, now. You must not say such things."

NOW THAT the outer barriers were won, the Black Knight and Cedric safely crossed the moat on a floating bridge. At the same time, amidst clouds of smoke, Ulrica raised the red flag.

Seeing the smoke, Guilbert shouted to the others, "All is lost! Someone has set the castle aflame."

De Bracy rushed to lower the drawbridge to escape. He was

XXXVI

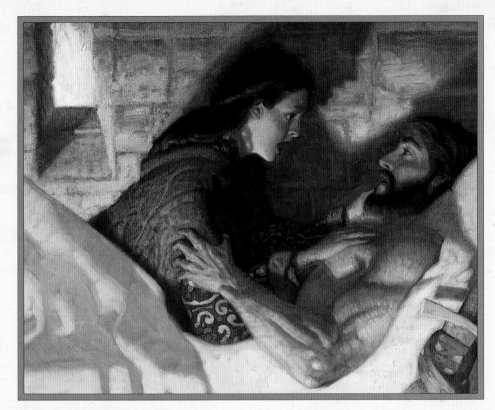

met by the Black Knight, and they fought furiously until at last
De Bracy fell.

"Yield, De Bracy," the Black Knight commanded.

"Not to an unknown conqueror."

The Black Knight spoke his name.

"Sire!" exclaimed De Bracy. "I yield, and give you my fealty."

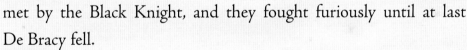HILE THE rescuers rushed to save the others, Guilbert burst
into the cell where Rebecca and Ivanhoe were. "Rebecca, I've
risked much to save you. Come with me now," demanded Guilbert.

"I will not leave Ivanhoe," insisted Rebecca.

Lifting her up into his arms, Guilbert declared, "It is not for you
to choose."

XXXVII

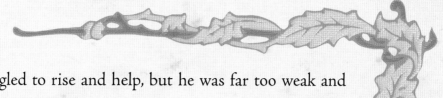

Ivanhoe struggled to rise and help, but he was far too weak and fell back on the bed, unconscious. Only moments later, the Black Knight entered the cell, which was now engulfed in flames. As he lifted Ivanhoe, the injured man revived briefly, begging the Black Knight, "There are others you must help. Leave me, and look to Rebecca and the lady Rowena."

"They are all safely away from the castle. Do not worry, my brave friend," said the knight as he carried Ivanhoe from the blaze. Behind them, stone and mortar crumbled, and for just a moment the solitary figure of Ulrica appeared standing on a turret. Triumphantly, she flung her arms wide, the turret gave way, and hungry flames consumed her.

THE OTHERS REJOICED to be saved, and before leaving the forest for home, Cedric vowed that should ever the Black Knight or Robin Hood wish for a boon he would gladly grant it. But Isaac was devastated to learn that his daughter had been carried away.

"My men saw Guilbert take her to Templestowe, the cloister of the Templar knights, and there we have no hope of rescuing her," Robin told him. "For we are too few and the cloister is well fortified against assault."

"I will go myself," said Isaac, "and offer any ransom in exchange for her." And so to Templestowe he went, with several of Robin Hood's men as guides.

XXXIX

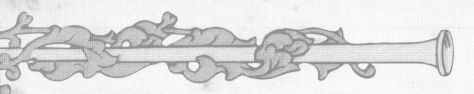

FTER IVANHOE'S RESCUE from the burning castle, he was taken to a priory. Once he was nearly recovered, the Black Knight rode with him to Cedric's castle. Before they passed through the gates, the Black Knight said, "Wrap your mantle around your face. It is best that your father not know that you have come to see him, till I have asked him for the boon he has promised me in exchange for his rescue."

When they stood before Cedric, Rowena, and her betrothed, Prince Athelstane, the Black Knight asked, "Do you remember, Cedric, that you promised to grant me a boon?"

"Aye," said the Saxon. "If it is within my power, it is granted before you ask."

"First, you have the right to know who asks for such a gift," said the knight, removing his helmet. "I am Richard the Lion-Heart, King of England. And, as far as what I wish, it is that you forgive your son, for a better knight has never lived. His bravery while fighting by my side in the Crusades was matched by none."

Ivanhoe stepped forward and said, "Father."

"My son," said Cedric, hesitating. And then, as he went to embrace Ivanhoe with tear-filled eyes, he continued, "I forgive you and hope that you too will forgive me for my rashness in condemning you."

Prince Athelstane came forward. "Cedric, clearly it is Ivanhoe that the lady Rowena loves. And so I must gladly give up my claim

to her hand in favor of your son." And then the prince led Rowena to Ivanhoe and clasped their hands together.

IT WAS NIGHTFALL when Isaac arrived at Templestowe seeking Guilbert. There he was brought to the Grand Master of the Templars. "What is your business with the Templar knight Bois-Guilbert?" the Grand Master demanded.

"I come to pay him any amount to release my daughter, who he is holding here," the merchant answered.

The Grand Master flew into a rage. "What is this sacrilege? It cannot be true that a woman is being held in this holy cloister by a Templar! Throw this man out. And kill him if he so much as shows his face here again," he commanded. Then he summoned the Abbot of Templestowe. "Is it true that Guilbert holds a woman here?"

The abbot knew that if he confessed the truth, he would bring ruin not only upon Guilbert, but himself as well for granting such permission. "If I have sinned by allowing him to bring her here, it was because I hoped to help break the spell she has cast upon him," said the abbot. "Our brother Guilbert is to be pitied, for he is suffering from a wild and unnatural devotion to this creature."

"Then she is a sorceress, who has bewitched our brother," concluded the Grand Master. "You have done well to bring the witch here. We will prepare for a trial at once. She will be judged, condemned, and burned as a witch."

The abbot rushed to warn Guilbert. When he told him of the Grand Master's plan, Guilbert objected violently. "This is madness! Rebecca is no witch!" he shouted.

"That may be, but we are all at risk if you try to shield her," said the other.

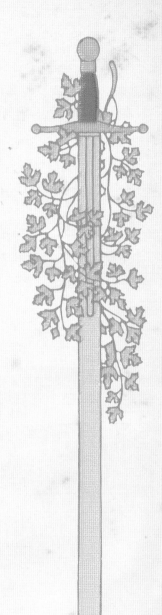

AT THE TRIAL—if a trial it could be called—Rebecca was tried and quickly convicted. But before the Grand Master could condemn her, Rebecca stood up and said, "By the rules of your holy order, I have the privilege to ask for trial by combat."

Guilbert had advised her to make such a request, knowing that she would not be refused. Under the rules of trial by combat, a champion would engage in battle with a Templar knight on

Rebecca's behalf. If Rebecca's champion won, it would prove that she was innocent of all charges, and she would go free.

Her request was granted, and she was given three days to wait for a champion to come forward. But, when Guilbert offered to be her champion, to his horror the Grand Master refused and instead chose him to uphold the Templars.

The next day Isaac received a message from Rebecca asking for his help. "There is only one noble enough to risk his life for my daughter. But I fear he is still too ill to help her," thought Isaac.

ACH DAY THAT PASSED, Guilbert fell more deeply in love with Rebecca, for her purity and courage forced him to reflect upon his own soul and to wish to be a better man. Over and over he pleaded with her to flee with him. But she never wavered from her firm refusal. "God will not let such injustice prevail," she insisted.

Finally, on the morning of the third day, Guilbert entered her cell to make one last plea. "It is my fault that you must face this peril. I shall never forgive myself if harm comes to you. Please, Rebecca, I beg you. Let me take you away. There is still time for us to escape."

"I will not run," said Rebecca. "I have put my fate in God's hands."

"Don't you see that you are sealing your own doom! Today you will be damned as a witch and burned." Yet she still refused.

XLIV

At the appointed hour, Rebecca was dragged out of her cell and the Grand Master announced, "Brian de Bois-Guilbert stands ready to do battle with any knight who will defend the accused. We will wait only until the shadows fall across the field. If no one presents himself, the witch shall be burned."

No one expected that a champion would appear on her behalf, and so Rebecca was tied to a stake and left to wait. Time slipped by in silence, and then, a solitary rider galloped slowly onto the field. "I am Wilfred of Ivanhoe," he said, "come to defend Rebecca."

Guilbert refused to fight. "This man is still recovering from wounds he sustained from a previous battle," he noted. "Surely he is too weak to do battle with me."

"If you do not fight," the Grand Master warned Guilbert, "you and the witch will be burned together."

In despair, the Templar reluctantly mounted his horse, and the two knights took their places. At the signal, they charged. Immediately, Ivanhoe and his horse went down, but Guilbert, though he had barely been touched, fell also. When Ivanhoe and the others went to him, they found Guilbert dead.

The Grand Master was forced to declare, "This is the judgment of the Lord. Rebecca is blameless of the charges and may go free."

IN THE DAYS THAT FOLLOWED, Ivanhoe and Rowena were wed. King Richard attended, having taken back his throne from his brother, John. Many Normans as well as Saxons joined in the peaceful marriage celebration, a sign of future harmony between the rival clans.

At the end of the festivities, Rebecca went to pay her respects to the bride. "I want to give you this gift, Lady Rowena, and to say farewell," said the maiden. "My father and I are leaving England for Spain."

"I wonder that you do not stay with us, for my husband will surely miss you if you leave," said Rowena, without a glance at the small silver box that Rebecca held out to her.

Rebecca stopped short and her eyes filled with tears for an instant. "No, lady, but I thank you. Among my people there are women who devote their efforts to good works, tending the sick, feeding the hungry, and relieving those in distress. Say this to your good husband if he should inquire after me."

Opening the box, Rowena saw a necklace and earrings of diamonds, which were of immense value. "I dare not accept such a precious gift."

"Keep it, please," insisted Rebecca. "Take these sparkling trifles as a small token of gratitude for my liberty."

Rowena blushed and was ashamed for ever feeling jealousy toward Rebecca. "Forgive me," she said. "My love for Ivanhoe is so

complete that up until now I could not imagine that you would not love him also."

"As the Lord is my judge, lady," Rebecca swore, "I know Ivanhoe loves only you. As for me, he has been a blessed friend."

Then she glided from the chamber, leaving Rowena as surprised as if an angel had visited her.

IVANHOE LIVED LONG and happily with Rowena, for they were attached by bonds of childhood affection, and they loved each other all the more for the obstacles that had once separated them. Ivanhoe distinguished himself in King Richard's service and was graced with much royal favor all the rest of his life. Yet it would be false to say that the recollection of Rebecca's beauty and courage did not come to him more frequently than the fair Rowena would have wished.

finis

A NOTE ABOUT SIR WALTER SCOTT

Born in Edinburgh, Scotland, in 1771, Sir Walter Scott acquired a level of fame, both socially and as a writer, that was nearly unmatched in his time. *Ivanhoe*, written in 1820, is Scott's most popular and best-known novel. Feeling that he had exhausted the familiar Scottish themes of his previous works, the author focused instead on the 12th century struggle between the Normans and the Saxons, creating a literary masterpiece that has influenced countless writers after him.

Scott was the innovator of the romantic-historical novel. By combining history and romance, he succeeded in making both remarkably vivid and beautiful. Although not always accurate historically, Scott's work has done more to boost our romantic illusion of the medieval age than any other writer in the English language. His novels, and in particular *Ivanhoe*, capture the essence of the era, and his descriptions of battles and knighthood, roving outlaw bands, and the Norman-Saxon conflict are especially compelling. Scott also drew inspiration from Shakespeare and Chaucer; as an example, his characters of Isaac and Rebecca are reminiscent of Shylock and Portia in *The Merchant of Venice*.

Scott loved the Scottish Lowlands, where he made his home at Abbotsford. There he lived like a feudal lord until death took him in 1832. His residence, now open to the public, contains a large library of 20,000 volumes collected by the author himself. Amidst family portraits there is a famous painting of Scott and his Scottish deerhound. In fact, in Edinburgh—on the road sloping toward Holyrood and Edinburgh castles—there is an imposing monument to Sir Walter, showing the illustrious writer standing beside his beloved dog.

AUTHOR'S NOTE

Sir Walter Scott's *Ivanhoe* significantly encouraged and defined my own powerful desire to write, illustrate, and design books. At the age of twelve, I was given a small, tattered 19th century facsimile edition with black-and-white woodcut illustrations. The idea of pictures in a volume of some length was a surprise to me; I don't think I had been aware that books with longer texts could be illustrated. And as I read Scott's vibrant narrative, a new genre in literature suddenly captured my imagination.

Now, years later, I hope to bring the story to an audience who may not have had a chance to be exposed to Scott's work. My picture book adaptation of *Ivanhoe* adheres closely to the original plot. Due to space constraints, certain scenes, subplots, and characters were omitted, but no key details were changed. This abridgment is meant as an introduction to and not as a substitute for Scott's extraordinary novel.